Lulu

Wishing Star

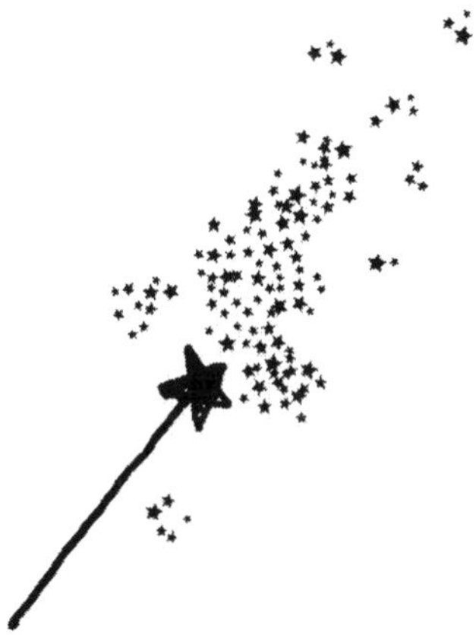

by Pippa Fern

Nanforde
PUBLISHERS

Published by Nanforde Publishers 2018
52 Wood End Avenue, Harrow, HA2 8NT, England

ISBN: 978-1-9993536-0-5

For Vilenka

Contents

1. The Wishing Star

'Sam'—Lulu turned to her big brother—'it's really weird! There's only one star for the whole of the sky tonight.'

'You are right, Lulu,' said Sam, peering towards the sky. 'That *is* the only star!'

It was just before bedtime, and Lulu and Sam were at the window, in their pyjamas, watching the night sky.

At that very moment, Mum walked into their room holding a tall pile of neatly folded laundry. It was so high they could barely see her nose.

'That's a Wishing Star,' Mum said, opening and closing drawers, 'the first star in the sky.' She had overheard Sam. 'It can make wishes come true,' Mum went on, rushing out the room, still holding Dad's half of the laundry. Mum was always busy.

'Wow!' said Lulu and Sam together, sitting up at once, like two springs. They started staring out the window at the Wishing Star, straightaway. As hard as they could. In complete silence.

Then the strangest thing happened.

'HAAAAIYAAAAA!'

Lulu and Sam were startled out of their wits by the loudest shrill voice. It was definitely not Mum's.

They turned around at once to face the trendiest lady they had ever seen, standing right in front of them.

The lady wore a shiny, tight-fitting pink pantsuit with high-heeled boots, and carried a bright green guitar across her back. Her hair was neatly styled with black and blue spikes that were almost as tall as the length of her face.

It's a rock star! Lulu thought.

The lady shimmered all over. Her entire outfit had glittery silver stars scattered all over it, which glowed like light bulbs. They turned to different colours from time to time.

Like a Christmas tree, thought Lulu—except that the lady was not plugged into a power socket.

Her boots were a beautiful sparkly purple, Lulu's favourite colour. They had really tall heels—way taller than those Mum wore to work. Lulu was amazed that the

lady managed to walk on them without toppling over.

Rock music was playing in the background now. *Strange,* thought Lulu and Sam—there was no stereo in their room.

BOOM, BOOM – BAM, BAM, the beat pounded, and every time the lady clicked her heels together, the tune changed.

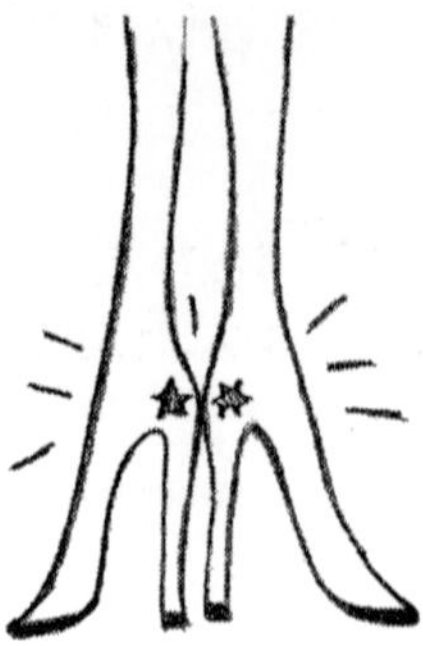

It was the strangest scene indeed.

Sam noticed that the bedroom door was still firmly shut—just as Mum had left it a minute ago.

The lady seemed to have appeared from thin air!

★

'Heellloooooo, helloooooooooo,' the lady greeted them again cheerfully, humming along to the latest tune in the background. Sam and Lulu just stared at her blankly, clearly bewildered.

'I'm Rock'n'roll-rockety-roo,' she said, beaming, and swayed to the music. 'I'm a fairy from the big Wishing star.' She skipped over to the window and pointed towards the sky.

'It's the coooooolest place, y'all,' the lady rattled on. 'I looooove chillaxing there, jamming my music—totally!' She stroked the fancy guitar that hung across her back. The guitar glowed brighter every time she turned.

It all sounded like gibberish to both Sam and Lulu. None of this made any sense. At all.

After what seemed like ages, Sam found his voice. 'So … you are a fairy?' he asked gingerly.

'Yah, mate … that I sure am,' the lady said, now fidgeting with her star-shaped

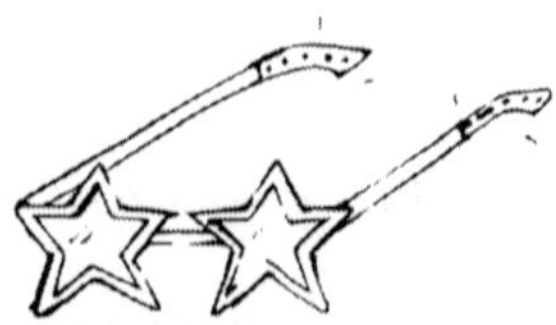

gold sunglasses. She kept putting them on and taking them off as she paced the room in a happy mood, grinning for no apparent reason. Every once in a while, she threw her head back, her chin up, and coiffed her perfectly styled hair.

'I was off to a rock concert on the other side of town when I got some signals on my Wish-o-meter from this direction.' The lady pulled a fancy gadget out of her pants pocket and peered at the screen.

'I had to stop—can't afford to miss any more homework,' she muttered, scowling.

Good grief! This is getting weirder still. A fairy who has homework?! Sam and Lulu rolled their eyes at each other in utter disbelief.

The lady was now busy tapping on the gadget, like Dad did with his fancy, expensive phone. 'Yes … my GPS *defo* says that the signals are from this house,' she said, nodding.

Defo must mean definitely, Lulu thought.

'Dad also has a GPS!' Sam whispered in Lulu's ear. 'It tells him which roads to drive on when—'

Hang on a minute, thought Sam. *If she needs a GPS to find her way, maybe the lady is no fairy after all!*

'If you are truly a fairy'—Sam folded his arms, looking sharply at the lady—'where is your gown? And your wings?' he

demanded, struggling to keep a steady voice. 'And your wand?' He had a whole string of questions to ask.

Sam was terrified. But he was not going to show it at all. Besides, he was Lulu's big brother, and it was his job to protect her. In all the books Sam had read, fairies always wore gowns, and the lady did not look like a fairy at all.

Lulu, however, sat quietly, continuing to stare at Rock'n'roll-rockety-roo.

'GOWN?' The fairy burst out laughing hysterically. 'Oooooooooh … you're soooo sooooo funny, yo!' she said in absolute stitches, pointing at a scowling Sam.

The lady makes a lot of 'Oooooo' sounds, thought Lulu. *And she talks funny, like*

Mason. Mason was their older cousin. He also called Lulu 'yo' sometimes.

'Gowns are sooooooo last year,' the fairy went on, wiping tears of laughter from her perfectly made-up face. 'The trend this season is pantsuits, yo! Totally!' she explained.

Neither Lulu nor Sam saw the joke or the explanation, but they listened to her anyway. Sam seemed to have run out of questions. He didn't chase after the wings or the wand.

'Oooooooooh… drat!' said Rock'n'roll-rockety-roo, glancing at her watch. 'I've got to run to catch the concert. Or, should I say … I've got to … fly! Ha haaaa haa.' She laughed at her own joke about flying.

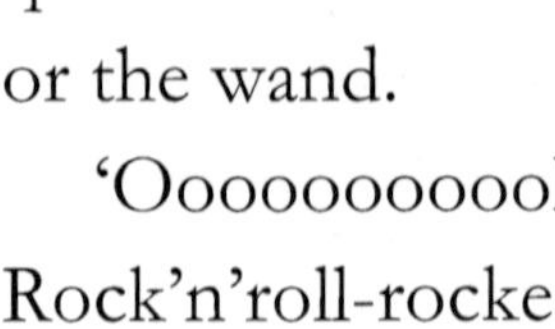

'The Bangers are on tonight, and I do not want to miss it for the world. They are my absoloooooooooot fave!' The fairy shut her eyes tightly to show how much she liked the group. Her eyelids were painted a beautiful pattern in glittery purple, pink, and silver. She had the longest eyelashes Lulu had ever seen.

She is stylish all right, Lulu thought.

'Now, dooooooooo let's get to business.' Rock'n'roll-rockety-roo looked harried and studied the Wish-o-meter again. 'The meter says two wishes were made. Both from this location. Am I right y'all?' she asked.

'The signals are terribly, terribly strong.' The fairy looked confused.

'Which can only mean... did you both make one and the same wish?'

Lulu and Sam looked at each other, as neither of them knew what the other had wished for, or whether they had made a wish at all. Everything had happened so fast.

'I wished to be able to walk,' Lulu piped-up, finding her voice. *The fairy looks friendly enough,* she thought.

'My wish, too, was for Lulu to walk,' Sam said sheepishly, 'so that I could play football with her.'

Sam and Lulu did everything together. They were the best of friends. But Sam could not play football with Lulu—and that was his favourite sport.

Lulu couldn't even walk, let alone play football. She just couldn't. 'Lulu's legs are not working properly,' Mum had explained to them when they asked her why. The doctors had told Mum this when Lulu was a baby.

Lulu went everywhere in her little wheelchair. She could wheel it herself, but Sam liked to push it. He wheeled her to school, to the park to play with their friends, to the shops, and to visit Grandma on Saturdays for tea.

At home, Mum and Dad carried Lulu everywhere—upstairs to bed, downstairs to the TV room, to the bath, and to the garden.

'Ooooh drat … ooooooh drat … oooooooh drat!' Rock'n'roll-rockety-roo shook her head. 'I am sooooo, soooooooo sorry, but that's beyond my school grade.'

Sam and Lulu were completely gobsmacked now. *There is a whole school of fairies?!*

'Working on humans, I mean,'—the fairy hung her head—'I crashed my last exam, so I can't work a wish like that. 'It's my bad, y'all. Totally,' she said. 'I spent sooooooo much time at concerts, I hadn't studied enough.'

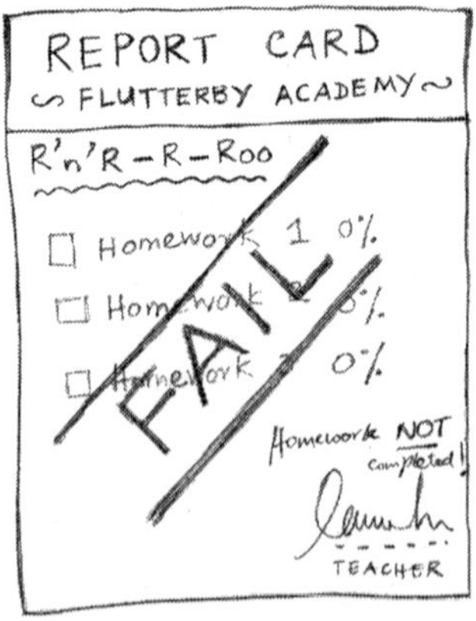

The fairy was now pacing the room, slowly, shoulders slouched and arms dangling by her sides. She looked worried and kept checking her watch from time to time. She was not humming anymore.

'Making wishes come true is hard work, y'all,' she muttered, more to herself than to Sam and Lulu. 'You *gotta* have your heart in it.'

Lulu and Sam just sat in silence, feeling sorry for the fairy. She was deep in thought and was walking faster and faster now. They felt dizzy watching her pace the room, back and forth, back and forth, back and forth.

After the longest time, Rock'n'roll-rockety-roo suddenly screeched to a halt, beaming from ear to ear. 'Oooooooh… I know it. I *know* it!' she yelled, leaping towards the ceiling as she snapped her heels in mid-air.

The music changed to an even faster beat.

BOOM-BOOM-BAM-BAM

BOOM-BOOM-BAM-BAM

'I cannot make you walk,'—she wagged her finger at Lulu—'but I sure can make you fly!'

2. Granting Wishes

Rock'n'roll-rockety-roo pulled her guitar to her front and broke into a lively tune. The guitar glowed brightly and turned to a golden yellow as she strummed. The beat in the background continued louder and faster than before.

BOOM-BOOM-BOOM

BAM-BAM-BAM

BOOM-BOOM-BOOM

The fairy swung the guitar about wildly and jumped up and down with her eyes closed—like a rock star would do on stage. She stamped her foot to the beat and swung her hips as wide as she could.

A sparkly purple and silver mist rose in swirls from the guitar, slowly filling the room.

Sam spotted a thin rod that was fixed to the end of the guitar, just where the swirls were coming from. 'That's surely a magic wand!' he whispered to an open-mouthed Lulu. But she was still as

stone and just kept staring at the fairy.

SWOOOOSH … SWOOOOOSH … SWOOOOOOSH

The fairy kept swinging her guitar in the air, again and again. She twisted and twirled, and bobbed her head up and down. Really hard.

Lulu and Sam could hardly see her through the purple-silver mist that was gathering in the room.

The fairy was kneeling on the floor now, her knees splayed, head thrown back, and pulling frantically at the guitar strings. 'OOOOOOH LA LAAA… THAT'S ROCKIN!' she screamed at interludes, breaking into tune. Her hair looked wild, and she huffed and she puffed.

At that very moment, Lulu and Sam heard Mum and Dad walk up the stairs. Any minute now, they could come into the room to tuck them into bed, as they did every night.

The fairy also looked worried. 'Ooooooooooohh … drat! I am running out of time!' She gasped, still swinging the guitar about, even more animated than before. She plucked the guitar strings even harder, and shrieked some more. 'YYYAAAAAAAAAAAAHEEEEEEEEE!'

Everything around the fairy shimmered and flashed brightly—like a giant sparkler—lighting up the room in

different colours. Lulu and Sam looked on, stunned, at all that was happening around them.

All of a sudden, the fairy stopped the ruckus and punched the air, whooping in joy. Lulu and Sam just held their breath.

'WOOOOOHOOOOO… y'all… it's done!' the fairy announced in absolute delight. 'I cannot make you walk, but I can *totally* make you fly!'

Rock'n'roll-rockety-roo made an elaborate bow to Sam and Lulu—just as a rock star would do on stage. But, her only audience was two astonished faces staring back.

The fairy, however, was clearly too chuffed to take any notice. 'TRALALALALAAAAA … another homework… done!' She skipped around the room in what seemed like an imaginary horse gallop.

'Working wishes is hard work, y'all,' she lectured Lulu and Sam as they stared at her quite blankly. 'You gotta have your heart in it!'

'Sam, Lulu… are you ready for bed?' It was Mum and Dad, and they were just outside the door.

'Ooooooooooooh, I've got to dash,' said Rock'n'roll-rockety-roo. 'Totally! Or should I say'—Lulu and Sam knew what was coming—'I've got to fly! Ha ha haaa.' The fairy grinned comically, blowing kisses in the children's direction.

And, POOF! She was gone. Disappeared into thin air. Just as she had appeared.

When Mum and Dad walked into the room, Lulu and Sam were still sitting at the window, quite speechless.

'It's time to go to bed, both of you,' Mum said, as Dad lifted Lulu from her chair onto her bed.

'Is it just me, dear, or does this room smell like bubblegum?' Dad asked Mum, looking around.

Only then did Sam and Lulu notice that, even though the purple-silver mist that filled the room had completely cleared, a sweet smell—like bubblegum—hung about in the air after Rock'n'roll-rockety-roo.

'Mum, Dad, you wouldn't believe what just happened,' Lulu started, but Sam shook his head, warning her not to say anything. Their parents would not believe what had just happened.

3. Flying Practice

When Sam and Lulu woke up the following day, they were both still puzzled by the strange events of the night before—unsure whether they were real or, in fact, all a dream.

They got ready for school, and, as usual, Dad carried Lulu downstairs and set her into her wheelchair.

They said goodbye to Mum and Dad, and Sam started pushing Lulu's wheelchair to school, as he did every day. At the end of their street was the park, and the school was just across from it.

'Lulu, can you remember anything odd about last night?' Sam asked gingerly the moment Mum and Dad were out of earshot, glad to have the chance to discuss the bizarre events of the previous night.

'Of course I remember the beautiful fairy, Rock'n'roll-rockety-roo.'

'Phew… I am glad. I thought I was going mad,' said Sam. 'If we both saw the same thing—a fairy with a guitar at that—it surely cannot be a dream!'

'Do you think I could really fly, Sam?' asked Lulu.

'That's what the fairy said, but the only way to find out would be to try!'

They obviously could not tell anyone else about this. It sounded crazy even to Lulu and Sam.

'But how?' Lulu looked confused. She hadn't grown any wings; she had checked very carefully. She didn't feel any different either. Lulu thought her big brother to be smart. *Surely he will know.*

The fairy had been in such a rush to leave before Dad and Mum came into the room that she didn't leave any instructions. At all.

'Rock'n'roll-rockety-roo really needs to study harder,' said Sam. 'I am sure fairies are meant to teach people how their wishes actually work.'

'Maybe there's a manual,' Lulu offered, 'like the one Dad read when he fitted the new TV.'

The park was deserted, and Sam wheeled Lulu under a big tree. 'Let me think now,' he said, chin in hand.

Lulu looked at her brother hopefully. *He looks wise,* she thought.

'We know that birds fly by flapping their wings,' said Sam. He had learnt all about it on a nature TV show. 'You don't have wings, Lulu, but maybe your arms will do. If you flap them really hard like a bird, if all goes well, you'll soon start flying. After all, the fairy did say you could fly now.'

Makes perfect sense, thought Lulu. She stretched her arms as far as she could and started flapping them.

'Oh, hang on—' Sam stopped her. 'You'd better take the belt off, or it could hold you down.'

'Good point!' said Lulu, unstrapping the safely lap belt in her wheelchair, and started to flap her arms again.

Sam watched her closely. 'Maybe a little faster, Lulu!' he cheered her on.

So, Lulu flapped and flapped and flapped her arms, as fast as she could, until they started hurting. But she was still firmly seated in her wheelchair, still under the big tree with Sam standing beside her.

'I think you are tired now, Lulu,' said Sam, checking his watch. 'Besides, we will be late for school.'

So off they hurried, both disappointed.

'To be fair,' Sam said after a while, 'the fairy did say it was hard work to make wishes come true. We will try again later, Lulu. It's only a matter of time till you fly.'

Lulu nodded in agreement.

★

Lulu and Sam spoke about flying all the time, but a whole week passed before they could try again. There were so many things to think about.

They couldn't fly in their back garden; either Mum or Dad was always there. They couldn't fly at Grandma's at the weekend; she lived in a top-floor flat, and

Lulu could fly straight out the window. It was way too risky. They couldn't practice in their bedroom; Lulu could hit the ceiling. Sam thought about every little detail.

The park was by far the safest place to practice. It was deserted most of the time, and there was plenty of space.

'Besides,' said Sam to Lulu, 'the soft grass lawn is perfect for landing.'

That whole week they walked through the park to school, but they always had someone else with them. There was Susie, the new girl in Lulu's class, and Dan, Sam's friend from football practice.

Sam and Lulu knew it was rude to avoid their friends, especially Susie, who didn't seem to have many friends at all. But they couldn't share their secret either. No one would believe them.

★

Sam thought of a plan.

The following Monday, they left for school early, before their friends did, and they stopped by the park.

'The other things we know to surely fly,' Sam reasoned confidently, 'are planes. Perhaps you have to take off like a plane does.'

'But how, Sam?' Lulu asked.

Sam wheeled her to the path in the middle of the park. It ran from one end of the park to the other. 'This is perfect,' he said. 'It's just like the runway at the airport.'

Lulu remembered watching planes take off at the airport while waiting for their flight to go on holiday.

'I will push you from one end to the other,' said Sam, 'and if all goes well, you will start flying just before the path ends. Just like the planes do.'

Lulu agreed, unfastening her lap belt. *This could work,* she thought.

'Hang on tight, Lulu!' Sam called, starting to push her wheelchair as fast as he could. Lulu wasn't scared. She was safe with Sam no matter how fast they went.

'Totally!' cried Lulu, 'just like Rock'n'roll-rockety-roo would say!' She sat in her wheelchair, her eyes closed,

arms outstretched, ready for takeoff. She even made a roaring sound, just for good measure.

'BHROOOOOOOOOMMMM…' That's what planes sounded like when they flew over their house.

But when Lulu opened her eyes, she was already at the end of the path and still firmly seated in her wheelchair. She hadn't taken off as planes do.

Sam and Lulu trudged to school slowly. Heads hanging. Feeling disappointed.

If only Rock'n'roll-rockety-roo had told them what to do, exactly.

4. The Terrible Three

The following day, Sam and Lulu couldn't leave for school early. Mum was running late to fix breakfast.

The moment they were out the door, Sam pulled a folded paper out of his trouser pocket. 'We have to have a plan,' he said, passing the paper to Lulu.

Sam liked to have a plan—for everything. He had neatly listed all the things he could think of that can fly.

~~Birds~~
~~Planes~~
Helicopters
Kites
Butterflies
Bees
Wasps
Hot air balloons
Rockets
Bats
Superman
Drones
....
....

The list went on and on. The top two items were already crossed off. Lulu knew why.

'If we knew how all of these things fly, Lulu,' Sam reasoned ever so confidently, 'we could try to fly like them, one by one. It has to be one of these ways.'

'But, Sam, butterflies, bees and wasps all use wings,' Lulu pointed out. 'Just like birds do.'

'Yes, maybe that's exactly what you need—a pair of wings!'

Lulu looked very worried now. 'Miss Spratt (she was their science teacher) said that butterflies live as caterpillars first and then inside a cocoon for weeks before they grow wings,' she said. 'I don't want to be in a cocoon.'

'Don't worry, Lulu. Rock'n'roll-rockety-roo would be silly to make you grow wings. She knows you have to go to school Monday to Friday. It's not even the holidays yet!'

'What you can do,' said Sam, 'is to wear something *like* wings. I will ask Mr. Maple to show me how to make a pair. He does craft lessons, so he should surely know.'

They were now half-way through the park, both deep in thought—about flying.

★

It was then that Lulu tugged at Sam's hand really hard. She looked petrified. Her face was as white as milk.

'Lulu! What's wrong?' Sam asked, his hand on her shoulder.

'Look, Sam, look!' Lulu pointed towards the edge of the park, trembling. 'It's the Terrible Three! Oh no… they've got Susie!'

Everyone in school knew of the Terrible Three—Charlie, Luke and Terrence. They were the oldest kids in school and the biggest bullies. The Terrible Three spared no one.

'We have to help Susie,' Sam said, more to himself than to Lulu.

Lulu was scared out of her mind. Her heart was pounding. Her head felt heavy. There were butterflies in her stomach—

but *not* in a good way. Even her knuckles had turned white. She wanted to cry.

Behind her, she heard Sam breathing heavily. He was craning his neck, looking all around the park for help, ideally for an adult. But no one was in sight.

Sam started wheeling Lulu slowly towards Susie. The three bullies now surrounded her. They could hear the ruckus clearly. Both Sam and Lulu knew they were heading for trouble—major trouble. But they had no choice. They could not leave Susie behind.

'You're such a baby!' taunted Charlie, the leader of the three. Susie was terribly upset.

'Stinky-Susie, silly-Susie, sloppy-Susie!' the Terrible Three chanted, laughing in her face.

'Hand me your lunch money… or else!' threatened Charlie while the other two sniggered. His face was just inches from Susie's. Luke was going through Susie's bag and throwing her books on the ground.

'I don't have any,' Susie whimpered, tears pouring down her face.

The bullies were so busy making fun of Susie they did not notice Lulu and Sam approach them.

'Oi! Let her go!' Sam shouted, trying hard to keep his voice steady. 'Keep cool, Sam!' he told himself, gripping Lulu's wheelchair. His knuckles had also turned white.

Lulu sat silently, without saying a word, her face still as white as cottage cheese.

The Terrible Three turned around at once, shocked to face Sam and Lulu. Then they burst out laughing. Really hard.

That was not quite the reaction Sam had been hoping for. But then, what *was* he thinking, picking on the Terrible Three? He had not thought this through. He started to panic.

'Oh, lookie who's here, mate!' Charlie sniggered, showing his big, yellow teeth. 'It's teeny-weeny, incy-wincy Sam! Trying to be a big-brave-boy now, are we, eh?' They laughed some more.

Lulu could not help but notice that Charlie liked using rhyming words. *This is hardly the time to spot poetry!* She shook her head, annoyed at herself. They were all in trouble. A lot of trouble.

Charlie was a burly fellow. Sam was Lulu's big brother all right, but he was no match for Charlie. He held Sam by the collar, almost lifting him off the ground. Sam looked terrified.

'Go, Lulu, go! Please get some help!' Sam yelled as Charlie shoved him into the blueberry bush next to the park bench.

'That will teach you not to meddle in our affairs, you puny-pimply-punk!' Charlie snarled.

His face looks a lot like Rover's, when he's angry, Lulu thought. Rover was the pit bull terrier next door.

Lulu took one look at poor Sam, now stuffed in the blueberry bush, and she started wheeling her wheelchair as fast as she could towards the park exit. She should meet an adult on the road, she willed.

'Oi, Terrence! Go… get her!' Charlie bellowed. 'At once! Who does that whingy-wheely-worm think she is?' Lulu heard him say.

Terrence was now chasing Lulu down the park path. She managed to catch a glimpse of Charlie pulling Sam again by the collar. Luke was towering over Susie.

They were all in real trouble. Only she could save them, Lulu knew.

5. Flying

Lulu wheeled her wheelchair as fast as she could, but Terrence was getting closer and closer.

'Focus, Lulu! Be brave!' Lulu told herself, over and over. 'Both Sam and Susie depend on you.'

Lulu's arms were hurting from all the wheeling, but she did not care. She wasn't even scared anymore. Helping Sam and Susie was all that she had in mind.

Lulu was now halfway to the park exit. She could clearly see the open gate and people walking on the street across. She was more determined than ever to get help.

But suddenly, everything started to go weird. Her wheelchair felt lighter. She didn't have to wheel it as hard as she had before.

It feels different, Lulu thought. *Very, very different.*

She couldn't see very well either. She peered over her shoulder, looking for Terrence. She couldn't see him—or anything else for that matter. Not the park, not where she was headed, not even her hands. She sat in a cloud of purple and silver mist. It kept growing thicker and thicker around her, covering her view of everything.

She felt her chair rise slowly. Or so she thought. It was all very confusing.

After what seemed like the longest time, the mist started clearing slowly. Lulu could see her hands now, and she held them in front of her face.

She felt two belts on her, strapping her firmly onto the wheelchair—one at her lap and one at her chest. They were bright green. *My wheelchair has only a lap belt,* Lulu remembered—clear as day. *And that is black!*

The wheelchair seat also felt very different. It was really soft, and Lulu felt like she was sitting on a huge marshmallow—not that she had actually sat on one, ever. And it was purple!

Lulu could not get her head around any of this.

She gingerly peered over her shoulder again, looking for Terrence.

'Holy moly!' Lulu gasped and slumped back on the plush purple cushion.

The clear blue sky and soft white clouds spread wherever she looked. A flock of birds flew so close to her that she could touch them, if she wanted to.

Lulu held onto the seat with both her

hands. It felt good to have the thick belts tightly in place.

In front of her stood a windscreen, similar to that in Dad's car. Down below, the park looked like a massive green carpet, scattered with green sponges that were actually the trees and bushes. The path Lulu had been on earlier stretched right across the park like a thick, grey ribbon.

This is the strangest dream, Lulu thought. *It has to be!*

She pinched her arm as hard as she could. 'OW!' she screamed. That hurt. *This is clearly no dream!*

'Inhaaaale…' Lulu murmured, taking a deep breath with her eyes tightly closed. 'Exhaaaale…' She blew the air out through her mouth, slowly. Very slowly. Just like Mum did at yoga. It was to calm her down, Mum had said. Calming down was exactly what Lulu needed now.

The weirdest of all was the control panel that had appeared in front of her. It had rows and rows of coloured buttons, like on a computer keyboard. They were labeled with different words. A purple stick with a glitter-ball head stood in the middle of the panel.

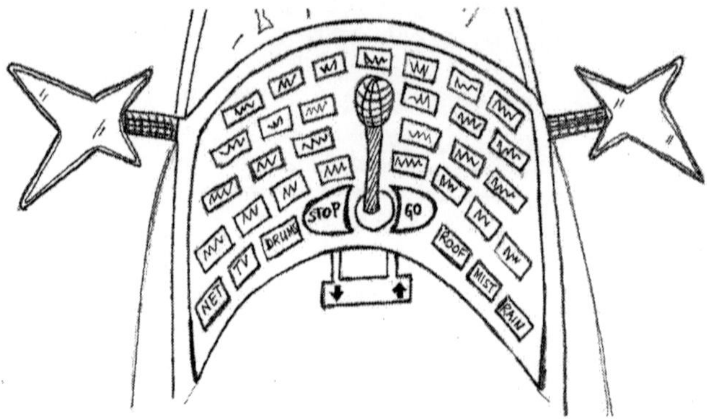

A large, green button marked GO was flashing, Lulu noticed in a daze. She didn't dare to touch any of the controls and continued to stare at them instead.

There was so much to take in for Lulu. Too much, in fact.

She pinched herself again, even harder than before, this time on the other arm. 'OUCH!' Lulu winced.

Lulu peered down, scanning the park for Terrence. He had stopped running and stood rooted to the ground like a pillar, staring up at her. He looked really silly with his eyes wide open and his lower jaw hanging.

Lulu wanted to pinch herself again, just to be sure, but changed her mind. The two bruises on her arms were proof enough. *This is definitely happening. For real!*

Lulu sat back with her eyes closed, and tried to clear her head. The breeze felt cool against her face. A sweet, strong smell hung about in the air—like bubblegum!

Lulu sat up abruptly. 'Of course it's not a dream,' she cried. 'It's Sam's and my wish come true!'

It was finally making sense. Well… sort of.

'I cannot make you walk…' Rock'n'roll-rockety-roo had said, Lulu remembered, *'but I sure can make you fly!'*

And here she was. Flying!

6. The Rescue

The wheelchair kept floating by itself slowly, towards the park exit—the same course Lulu had been wheeling on before everything went crazy.

Where were Sam and Susie? Lulu wondered, looking around, really worried for them.

Lulu spotted Sam at a distance. He was also running towards the park exit, all the while looking up in her direction. He looked tiny, like a wind-up toy soldier.

I have to get to Sam, thought Lulu, reaching for the wheels on either side, as she would usually do in her wheelchair. But nothing was usual today. The wheels were nowhere to be seen, and two dark blue, velvety surfaces sat in their place instead. They were decorated with tiny white stones that glittered, like the stars in the night sky.

How on earth am I to steer this towards Sam? Lulu wondered as she stared at the panel in front of her, trying to make sense of all the buttons. There were so many.

Lulu wasn't good with gadgets at all—she could barely manage the TV remote at home. Lulu wished Sam were there. *He would have known what to do,* she thought. *He always does.* She shook her head several times—as if that were going to make things clearer somehow.

Lulu took a deep breath and reached for the glitter-ball stick. She held it gently with both hands. *It looks a lot like the joystick Sam uses to drive the car in his video game,* she thought. Immediately, a purple beam flashed through the stick, and the glitter-ball started glowing brightly.

Lulu held her breath and slowly moved the stick slightly to the left. The wheelchair—*or whatever this is,* Lulu thought—glided gently to the left. When she moved the stick to the right, the chair shifted direction again.

'Phew… that wasn't too difficult!' said Lulu, starting to steer the chair slowly towards Sam. She felt a lot calmer than before.

'Lulu! Lulu! This way!' Sam yelled, waving madly at her. He had stopped running now and stood right below where the chair was flying.

Lulu gingerly pressed the big, red button marked STOP. *This has to be the one!* The chair cruised smoothly to a halt and started hovering about, still in the air. It showed no signs of landing.

Lulu could not find any button that said LAND, or anything similar. There were a whole lot of them—NET, ROCKS, TV, DRUMS, TURBO, ROOF, MIST, RAIN, CANDY, BONES… the buttons went on and on. One of them even had ICE CREAM printed on it.

The chair did look fancy indeed. Two guitar-shaped mirrors stood on either side of the windscreen—Lulu could see more sky behind her in the reflection. It even had heavily decorated speakers with ROCK'N'-ROO written boldly across them. Lulu rolled her eyes, thinking of Rock'n'roll-rockety-roo's madness for rock music.

Just below the panel was a lever with arrows pointed up and down printed on it. *This could work,* Lulu thought, pushing the handle down slowly. The chair swayed softly from side to side and touched down smoothly on the park lawn.

As soon as it parked, the word FLY-ROO appeared right across the windscreen in large, luminous, multi-coloured letters. *So, that's what my wheelchair has become,* Lulu thought. *Whatever a Fly-roo is!*

★

'Lulu, you're flying!' Sam beamed, running towards her. 'You figured how to, all by yourself. I'm so proud of you.'

'Er… I didn't do anything special, Sam,' Lulu replied. 'The wheelchair just started flying by itself, really.' Sam looked confused but said no more.

'Are you OK? Did Charlie hurt you?' asked Lulu.

'I'm fine. I ran as fast as I could. A few scratches on my arms from being shoved into the bush, but nothing major. But poor Susie is still in trouble.

'Charlie went back to her after I got away. He and Luke were still harassing her. I escaped to get help.'

'What about Terrence?' Lulu asked. 'He stopped chasing me—'

'Not sure what happened to him, Lulu. He bolted out of the park, looking as white as a sheet—as if he had just seen a ghost.'

'I know what happened,' Lulu said, as she burst out laughing. 'It was not a ghost he saw, but me—starting to fly!'

'Oh, well done.' Sam patted his sister's hand proudly. 'It serves

Terrence right, for being the bully he is!'

'The wheelchair is really neat, Lulu,' Sam said, inspecting it. 'It spits fire when flying—like a mini rocket—did you know?'

Lulu had no clue how the wheelchair flew. It had no wheels—that much she knew. So, it was not a 'wheelchair' anymore! It was all a blur. And she was still sat inside the chair, firmly held by the two green belts.

'We have to hurry, Lulu,' Sam said, sounding worried. 'Susie is still in trouble.'

'Let's fly, Sam. Can you perch at the back?' Lulu asked. There was no room for him on her seat. She was snuggly strapped in.

'It won't be safe.' Sam shook his head. He always thought about safety before doing anything.

'Oh, hang on—' said Sam, taking a closer look. 'Actually, there is a step for me to stand on.' He carefully stepped onto the platform at the back, quite chuffed at the thought of flying. Two large, green belts immediately snapped into place, holding him firmly against the backrest of the chair.

'Rock'n'roll-rockety-roo has done a fantastic job, Lulu,' said Sam. 'She has thought of everything. Hope she gets an A-plus on this homework.'

'Hold on, Sam!' Lulu hollered, as the chair rose elegantly towards the sky.

We are flying! Sam beamed. He wanted to pinch himself, just to be sure, but he was holding onto the chair with both hands, as tightly as he could.

They breezed gently across the park, the sweet smell of bubblegum wafting behind them.

★

'There they are!' Lulu pointed, expertly steering the Fly-roo towards Susie.

Charlie had his back to them, but both Susie and Luke spotted the Fly-roo in the sky.

Poor Susie could not get her head around what was going on. *The day is steadily getting worse,* she thought sadly. *First bullies, and now aliens?!* Her head was spinning. She just stared blankly, her face as white as snow.

Luke, on the other hand, recovered very quickly and legged it as fast as he could without a word of warning to Charlie.

'What a horrible friend Charlie has got,' Sam said to himself, watching the whole scene unfold from the sky.

Charlie continued chomping happily on Susie's sandwich. He was still facing away from Sam and Lulu. He didn't even care that Luke was legging it. He had Susie's lunchbox in one hand and the half-eaten sandwich in the other.

'Here we go, Sam!' Lulu lowered the Fly-roo, but not quite to the ground. It was now hovering just above Charlie's and Susie's heads.

'If I get off, Lulu, Charlie will punch me again,' Sam said. He was not taking any more chances.

Charlie was stuffing another sandwich in his mouth when he, at last, saw the Fly-roo. It was still in the air, hovering just above his head.

Charlie froze. His eyes almost popped out of their sockets—like two ping-pong balls. His mouth was gaping so wide that Lulu could see chunks of the half-eaten sandwich.

'Eeeeeww… that's gross!' Lulu said, as she stuck her tongue out in disgust.

'So, what shall we do?' Lulu asked.

'I know exactly what!' said Sam, grinning. 'Lower the chair a little more, Lulu.'

Without another word, Sam reached out and held Charlie tightly by his collar. 'Let's fly, Charlie boy!' he shouted, beaming from ear to ear.

'WHOOOAAAAAA!' cried Charlie. The chair swung to the side, slightly off balance with Charlie's weight.

'Where are we flying to, Sam?' Lulu asked, steadying the Fly-roo expertly.

'Straight to the old duck pond,' Sam yelled back. His hand was straining under Charlie's weight.

Charlie hung onto Sam's hand as hard as he possibly could. He hadn't quite come to his senses yet.

'This is crazy, man,' Charlie mumbled to himself. He was being carried by the skimpy-scrawny-Sam and his wheely-worm-sister. And… they were flying!

'You gotta be kidding me!' Charlie cried, baffled. *This has to be a nightmare!* He wanted to pinch himself to wake up, but he dared not let go of Sam's hand—just in case.

Charlie started bawling like a baby, tears pouring down his chubby cheeks. He begged Sam not to let go of him.

'Don't you worry, Charlie boy!' Sam chuckled. 'I won't let go…' He winked at Charlie. 'Not yet, anyway.'

'PLLEEEEEEEEAAAASE… Saaaaam,' Charlie wailed. 'I promise not to bully anyone. Ever. Or call names. Or steal lunches. Or scare them. Or shove people in bushes…' He went on and on. 'I will be on my best behavior. Please, Sam, pleeeeaaaaaaaaase.'

Sam felt sorry for him. He really did look like a gigantic baby now. He stopped blubbing only to spit out chunks of Susie's sandwich that were still stuck in his mouth.

But feeling sorry is not an option, Sam reminded himself. This was their only chance to make sure that Charlie and his gang stopped bullying everyone at school.

The old duck pond at the edge of the park did not have any ducks anymore. It was just a large, smelly, disgusting puddle of mud.

Lulu read Sam's mind and slowly lowered the chair towards the mud patch.

'Remember to keep all the promises you made, Charlie boy!' said Sam, gently lowering Charlie right in the middle of the muck.

SPLLAATT!

Charlie landed on his bum, splashing mud everywhere, still bawling.

'I promise! I promise! I promise!' Charlie moaned in between sniffles. He struggled to stand up but kept slipping in the mud over and over again. He was now coated head to foot in layers and layers of disgusting slime. Only his eyes could be seen, sticking out like two shiny marbles.

Sam and Lulu couldn't help laughing as they began to fly towards Susie.

'The big bully Charlie—the leader of the Terrible Three—looks like a massive chocolate bunny,' said Lulu, chuckling. 'Not so scary now!'

'Susie, are you OK?' Sam hollered as they approached her, while still in the air. Lulu waved hard, smiling.

Susie did not smile back. Or wave. Her face was still as white as milk. She gathered her things as quickly as she could and started running towards the school.

'Who can blame her?' said Sam. 'The poor girl must be having the worst day of her life.'

Lulu agreed.

7. Going Home

'What now, Sam?' Lulu asked. 'We have to get to school.'

'I think I have to change before that,' said Sam, trying to wipe the dirt off his uniform. He looked a right mess indeed.

'Mrs Gooseberry will not be best pleased to see you like that,' Lulu said. She was Sam's teacher.

'Let's fly home, Lulu,' Sam said, checking his watch. 'I can change quickly and still get to school on time—if we hurry.'

'Mum and Dad might still be there,' Lulu said. 'We can show them the Fly-roo.'

'Is that what it's called, Lulu?' Sam asked.

'I think so. The letters F-L-Y-R-O-O appeared on the screen when I landed earlier,' Lulu said, spelling the word out for Sam, 'but now it's gone.'

'Sounds like Rock'n'roll-rockety-roo, I guess,' said Sam, smiling.

The chair floated across the park and over the houses. Their street looked really pretty from above—a neat row of houses with matching back gardens.

They all look alike, thought Lulu. *Like the little plastic houses in the Monopoly set.*

'It's right there, Lulu!' Sam shouted, peering down. 'That's our house! I can see the trampoline, the garden shed, and my bike!'

'I can see Dad's car in the driveway!' said Lulu.

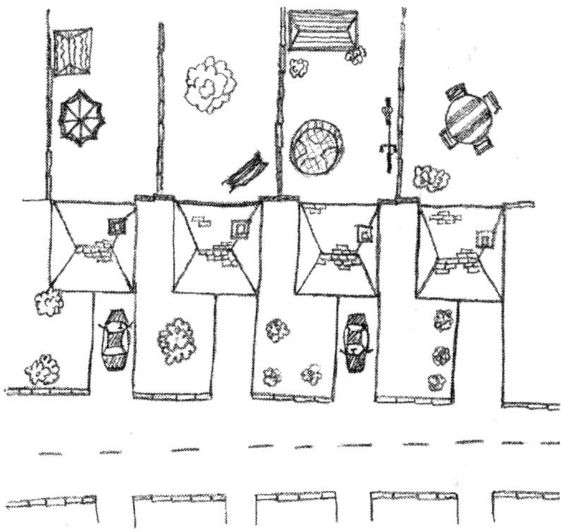

After hovering above their house for a minute or two, Lulu gently lowered the Fly-roo onto the front porch. She was becoming an expert in flying. Sam was proud of his little sister.

'I'll be back in a jiffy,' said Sam as he jumped off the Fly-roo and ran into the house.

'Sam?!' Mum jumped, startled, with her hand on her chest. Sam had bumped into her as soon as he opened the front door. She was not expecting to see him back home at this time of the day—certainly not in the way he looked now.

'What happened to you?' she demanded, looking very worried. 'Where's Lulu?

'Bradley! Come here, quickly!' Mum shouted for Dad.

'Please don't worry, Mum—' Sam

tried to calm her down.

'Oh my word, Sam!' Dad cut in, his eyebrows furrowing under his glasses. 'What on earth happened to you? Where is Lulu?'

'Please don't worry. Lulu is fine,' Sam said. 'She is on the front porch, waiting for me.' Both Mum and Dad relaxed a little.

'Charlie pushed me into a bush at the park, and—' Sam offered to explain, still trying to rub the dirt off his school jumper.

'It's not like you to get into fights, Sam,' Mum interrupted, scowling.

'I didn't, Mum,' Sam said. 'Charlie and his friends

were bullying Susie in the park, and Lulu and I had to help her. We just had to. There was no one else around.'

'I am going to call Mr Potts right away,' Dad declared, already marching towards the phone. Mr Potts was the school headmaster.

'Dad, please don't!' Sam pleaded. 'Please. Charlie promised not to bother anyone again. Ever.' Sam didn't want Charlie to get into trouble with the headmaster. After all, he had promised to behave properly hereafter.

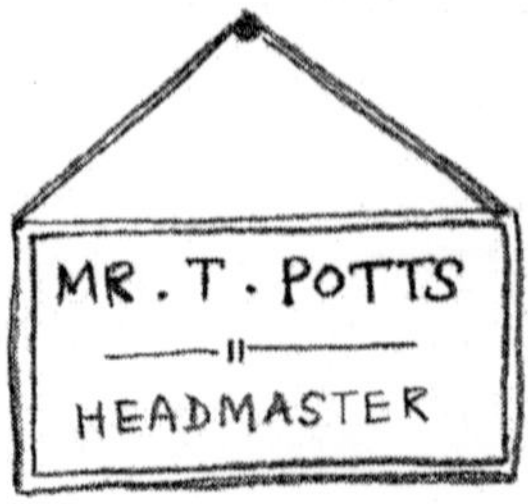

'And why on earth would Charlie promise you that?' Dad raised his eyebrows, looking very skeptical.

'You *have* to believe this, Mum, Dad…' Sam looked from one to the other. 'Lulu can fly in her chair now!' he said, almost in a whisper.

'We saw Charlie, Terrence, and Luke bothering Susie—we rescued her—lifted Charlie in the air—dropped him into the old duck pond—he's not hurt at all—just scared and promising to behave—and Terrence and Luke just ran off leaving Charlie behind!' Sam said, all in one go. Then he took a deep breath.

For a moment, which seemed like a very long time to Sam, Mum and Dad just stared at him and then at each other.

The furrow in Dad's forehead was steadily deepening. His left eyebrow was now clearly touching the right one, Sam noticed, worriedly.

Mum was at a complete loss for words. Sam had never seen that happen before. Ever. She just stood there, her hand on her chest and mouth wide open.

'Hang on, Sam, slow down…please,' Dad started, holding Sam firmly by his right shoulder. 'Just to be clear…'

Sam sighed in relief that one of them had found their voice, finally.

Dad peered into Sam's face, his nose almost touching Sam's.

'Are … you … saying … that … Lulu … *flies* … in … her … wheelchair?' He said the words very slowly, one by one, with long pauses between them—as if Sam wouldn't understand if Dad spoke at his regular speed.

'That's right, Dad!' Sam said, 'That's exactly what I'm saying.' He was glad that at least Dad was coming to his senses.

Mum, on the other hand, just stood there, just as before, hand on her chest and mouth still wide open.

'Fairy Rock'n'roll-rockety-roo granted Lulu's and my wish,' Sam said. 'Well, sort of.' Now was certainly not the time to explain to Dad about Rock'n'roll-rockety-roo's poor exam grades—and the concerts! After all, that was why Lulu was flying instead of walking.

'We wished for Lulu to walk.' Sam fidgeted with his fingers. 'The fairy couldn't make that happen, but Lulu can now fly instead.' He kept talking steadily, looking only at Dad. Mum didn't seem able to function anymore. 'In her chair, with me standing at the back,' Sam finished explaining.

'Let's go to the porch and check the chair out, Dad,' Sam said. 'It's called a Fly-roo. It's really the coooooolest thing you have ever seen. Ever!'

Dad threw a confused look at Mum and wiped his brow. He looked sweaty. *That's strange,* Sam thought. *It was quite cool inside the house.*

'And, Dad—' Sam was impatient to tell him about all the nifty gadgets the chair had too.

'Hang on, Sam,' said Dad firmly. 'Let's just find Lulu before we hear anything more.' He headed to the porch. Mum followed Dad—a bit like a robot, still in complete silence.

'Hello, darling,' Sam heard Dad say.

Then silence.

Sam thought it was strange that he couldn't hear Lulu's excited chatter in showing the Fly-roo to Mum and Dad.

When Sam stepped out the door, he was not prepared for what he saw, at all.

Lulu sat on the porch in her old, black wheelchair, with Mum and Dad on either side of her, holding her hands.

'It's gone, Sam,' Lulu said, softly. 'It just disappeared.' She shrugged.

'Mum, Dad,' said Lulu, 'Sam and I were flying on the Fly-roo. We saved Susie from Charlie and his gang and flew home in it. It just turned back into my old wheelchair a minute ago.'

'Yes, honey,' said Dad, smiling broadly as he rubbed the top of Lulu's head. 'Sam told us *all* about it.' He stretched on the 'all' for far longer than necessary before throwing a knowing look at Mum. They both rolled their eyes at each other and shared a puzzled smile.

'Well, you both best be hurrying to school,' Mum announced—she had found her voice again. 'Sam, there is a fresh sweater in the drawer.'

It was Sam who was speechless now. He ran upstairs, his cheeks as red as cranberry juice. *Mum and Dad must think we are mad,* he thought.

If they did, they did not show it. They said goodbye to Lulu and Sam for the second time that day. Sam sheepishly started pushing Lulu's wheelchair as Mum and Dad waved from the porch.

'Is it just me, dear, or does it smell like bubblegum?' Sam and Lulu heard Dad ask Mum.

★

'What just happened, Lulu?' Sam looked completely confused.

'I have no clue.' Lulu rubbed her forehead. 'It just turned back to the old wheelchair as soon as you went indoors.'

'But how did it all start?' asked Sam, trying to make sense of it all. 'What did you do to make the wheelchair fly in the first place?'

'I don't know, Sam,' said Lulu, deep in thought. 'There was no time to think anything through. The only thing on my mind was saving you and Susie. I wasn't even scared; I just wanted to help you, no matter what.'

They both walked for a long time, in silence, across the park and towards the school.

'Maybe it's just that, Lulu!' Sam said softly. 'Maybe it was your courage and your need to help us that got the chair flying. You put us before yourself. You were very brave.'

'Making wishes come true is hard work, y'all … you gotta have your heart in it!' Rock'n'roll-rockety-roo had said, Sam remembered.

'When will we be able to fly again, Sam?' Lulu asked.

'I don't know, Lulu. We will have to wait and see.'

★

That night, the same as every other, Sam and Lulu sat at the window to watch the night sky. A blanket of stars glittered—like diamonds.

'One of those has to be the Wishing Star,' Sam said, as Lulu nodded in agreement.

'Thank you!' they mouthed together towards the sky, grateful for their day of adventure.

Rock'n'roll-rockety-roo must be in her pad, jamming her music, they thought. *'That's cooooooool, y'all. Totally!'* they imagined her to say.

★ The End ★

16295819R00062

Printed in Great Britain
by Amazon